THE ART OF BEING DIFFICULT

A NOVELETTE BY WILLIAM CHEKHOV

MENDELSSOHN PRESS

The Art of Being Difficult

A Novelette by William Chekhov

Copyright 2024

Mendelssohn Press

16410 Riggs Rd

Stilwell, KS 66085

Library of Congress Control Number: 2024905333

WARNING: CONTAINS TRIGGERS

WARNING: NSFWAE (NOT SAFE FOR WORK OR
ANYWHERE ELSE)

WARNING: UNSAFE AND INEFFECTIVE

WARNING: MISINFORMATION

WARNING: CERTIFIED UNDEMOCRATIC

WARNING: HAZARDOUS TO ENVIRONMENT

WARNING: MAY CONTAIN GLUTEN

TLDR

Kotan's mother (Mujaki) dies giving birth to him. His father never forgives his wife for not aborting her baby, and despises his son for taking his mother's place. Kotan's classmates and coworkers likewise deride him, and once he is even fired without a cause. He bounces around at different jobs, but never finds satisfaction or fulfillment. He feels inadequate and unworthy of love, so he "saves" Inyoku from a brothel and falls in love with her. She marries him for his money. Despite his best efforts, she has contempt for him, and constantly cheats on him. Kotan finds out she is pregnant and orders her to abort the baby. She refuses. Meanwhile, he loves his best friend, and the feeling is mutual. But instead of leaving his wife for her, he murders his wife, her current paramour, and finally himself. The father realizes his behavior put a curse on his family.

WARNING: CONTAINS SPOILERS

WARNING: CONTAINS SPOILERS

To every friend I wish I could love more

CHAPTER 1

They all watched him. Silvester slowly licked his lips; Sydney breathed deeper than usual; her conspicuous breasts gently rose and fell; Sam circled his thumb against his middle and pointer finger, imagining it was circling something else. Sarah admired Sydney's breasts from her periphery, longing for them forever.

Kotan slipped.

It was messy.

He hit his head and passed out, a success that thrust his colleagues into deep ecstasy. Sydney frantically grabbed her phone and googled if it still might work? Sarah burned with envy; Silvester clenched and pumped his fist; Sam chuckled nervously; Kotan woke up in the hospital.

CHAPTER 1.1

"Customer 42, your order is ready."

CHAPTER 1.2

"Those big countries scare me. Like Ch— and Ru— ...."

"I never thought she would end up with someone like him...."

"He was dying, and the hospital would not even let him...."

"She donated her hair, but..."

"So she started dating this guy she is working with. Everybody is freaking out because she is 21, and he is 30..."

His favorite part of the job was eavesdropping. He loved learning tidbits from the lives of others. He understood the most casual conversations revealed more about life than the most intimate moments of luxury.

And he knew he would never have the latter.

He knew he could never love or be loved.

So he looked for something else in life.

He never knew what he looked for, but to be alive was to be seeking something. It was to grasp for something, to long for something....

CHAPTER 1.3

He bustled about. The glasses on the tray rocked wildly. His forehead glistened; daggers blinded him. His blistery feet burned.

"Table 6!"

Kotan wheeled around and rushed to the southeast corner.

"Excuse me, sir. Could I get another spoon? I dropped mine."

He bowed eloquently.

"Table 6, Kotan! I SAID TABLE 6 !!! "

"We need a salt refill when you get the chance."

"Hai !"

"Kotan! The trash is full in the back."

"Hai !"

His face grew flushed, and the skin seemed to tighten around his eyes.

It was messy.

CHAPTER 2.1

"Customer 42, your order is ready."

CHAPTER 2.2

For sinful reasons Sydney visited him in the hospital.

He woke up, descried her shadowy figure in the gloom, and felt her love.

He mumbled incoherently.

She leaned over, gently touched his thigh — slightly more inside than necessary — and shushed him.

He tried to sit up and silently howled. His face disfigured.

Vinegar please.

Yes, yes... of course...

Her hand slipped almost unnoticeably.

Hospital dress was simple. A thin, scratchy robe.

The door opened.

Narrow rescue.

CHAPTER 3.1

"42….. Paging customer 42…."

CHAPTER 3.2

A woman approaches, holding her phone in front of her, griping at an unseen guest.

"Yeah, yeah... well... if you... hold on... I will take the broccoli cheese... yeah, yeah..."

"Would you like that with bread?" Kotan asked sheepishly, torn between interrupting and doing his job.

"Yeah, yeah... well I think if he does it, he needs to run the numbers by Geoffrey...."

Kotan waited.

"Yeah... yeah..."

He gently cleared his throat. "Would you like that with bread?"

Slightly more assertively.

"Yeah... yeah... well he really needs to step up... Frank cannot do it all..."

She nods. "Good idea..." looking askance at Kotan, tapping her card, thoroughly and impressively ignoring him.

Kotan turned glum.

The next one has a bright smile, refreshingly present

with lots of eye contact. After pleasantries, the phone rudely interrupts.

"Ah, excuse me."

He is dreadfully apologetic. Fumbles with his phone. It rings and rings and rings, while he peers at with profound confusion as if meeting a talking squirrel for the first time. "Hello? Ahhhh yes! Good to hear from you!"

....

"Yeah... yeah..."

"Would you like that with bread, or..."

"Yeah... yeah... I think we could make that work. Go ahead and shoot me an email and CC Pamela..."

"Would you like that...."

"bread..."

His voice trailed off, as he noticed the next person in line was on the phone. He went down the line and blanched.

Life was hopeless.

Two minutes later he apathetically welcomed another teleconversationalist.

It was a serious conversation.

Three minutes later, a man apologized, pulled out a phone and called his wife.

"Yeah... yeah.... so what did you want? Hmmmm..."

"Are you sure?"

"Well, they have broccoli cheese... squash... lobster bisque..."

He read the entire menu.

"No, no... BROCCOLI cheese!" He was exasperated.

The line trailed out the door.

Kotan's mind wandered past them all into the forest. But the forest was dark, and he got lost.

There were no breadcrumbs.

CHAPTER 4.1

"Customer 42... your food is getting cold...."

CHAPTER 4.2

Kotan never cared about the future. Why look at a hopeless future? He would die soon, before Bloody Mary returned; any day.... crumple to the ground... die... If that failed, he knew the world would end soon. These days everybody sat around and waited for the apocalypse. All the movies prophesied post-apocalyptic life, and they were no longer consumed as fiction, but as future reality.

His retirement plan was to die young.

He never once considered living a normal life span.

He had nobody to give money to, nobody to saddle with his copious debt. They could only hurt him until he was dead.

Better to die with debt than with profit. No greater sin than to die with unspent money.

CHAPTER 5.1

Customer 42 sat on the toilet. He felt anxious as he faintly heard his name called in the main room.

But he could do nothing.

When he returned home, he would eat four or five prunes. In the meantime, he scrolled through social media propaganda, and slowly became a communist...

CHAPTER 6

A single handwritten quote was scribbled above his bed:
"What you believe about money defines your life."

CHAPTER 6.41

"Customer 42, get your a-- over here, please."

CHAPTER 7

The elderly woman brought her soup to the counter.

Her nose wrinkled, then flared.

"The soup is thinner than usual." She hissed.

Kotan remembered the same woman complained about the coffee last week.

With profound admiration he realized she was a master of complaint.

He bowed respectfully.

CHAPTER 7.1

"Customer 42, this is your last f------ chance."

Her tone was friendly and cordial.

One was never judged not by what they said, but by how they said it.

With a voice like that, she would never be judged.

CHAPTER 8

The man objected.

"I gave you 43."

Kotan shook his head firmly, but a little sadly.

"It was 42."

"I know it was 43." He snarled.

Fake smile.

"No worries, sir."

Just another day... ♫

CHAPTER 9

Kotan shot by a 50 sign at 85. A car whipped by him at 100.

Another sign.

"Speed limit strictly enforced."

He realized with a pang that nobody respected the law anymore.

Not even himself.

CHAPTER 9.1

Kotan was impressed.

"What did you get? It looks amazing."

She shrugged.

"I don't know... But it has avocados."

She sounded hopeful.

Millennials love avocados.

Kotan decided he liked her.

Anybody that loved avocados would make a good friend.

And the sex would be amazing.

CHAPTER 9.2

Suddenly the doors burst open, and men with assault rifles rush in and gun down a man seated at a table. He's screaming and gushing out blood as they drag him out.

Nobody so much as twitches.

Nobody notices. Whoever notices is next.

Frank is speaking softly with Sally. "Been a little chilly the last two days."

"Yeah, I'm ready for Summer."

They slowly sip their ginger beer.

Their hands slightly tremble.

Sally kindly excuses herself to the restroom, where she throws up, and returns to the table.

"Where were we?" She asks sweetly.

"I think we were talking about love."

"Ah."

She appeared thoughtful.

"What's that?"

"I can show you."

"How?"

Frank, so full of passion, could hardly speak. He looked at her desperately, hoping that somehow, someway, she understood that which could never be said.

CHAPTER 9.3

"So that will be a turkey sandwich with bre -- "

"I'll have bread with that!" She snapped viciously.

"And a dr -- "

"And a drink!" She vociferously added, just in time...

"Would you like a r -- "

"And I want my receipt!" She growled like Moufasa.

Kotan was ready to die.

CHAPTER 10

A narrow crack, less alley than accidental space, like the crack in American bathroom stalls. People pause until they descry the hint of Presence, and move on silently through the misery. Contortion, the only way through, and nobody had that Imagination, save one, who glided through like the shadow of a doe. Blackness swallowed her. A faint suggestion of warmth; deeper gloom; voices. The distinct and deliberate crack of stilettos on wood; near silent rustle of silk; sticky smell of cheap perfume; tacit but poignant attitude: nobody deserved better. Another hallway. Fatuous feminine laughter; insecure braggadocia. Finally a mirror: deep violet; the lips the same; and somehow the eyes... but for a moment...

A room of fakes, the kind built with money — nothing else. No future; no past. Underneath this scene a girl slept for the 1346th day. For three years she wondered about the weather; sometimes about the soul; after which she knew there were neither. Silent and unnoticed *Parasite.*

Or *Worm.*

A month later she would grow ill and die. She would be discovered by another girl subconsciously following her nose, who would frantically (half) whisper to another, and yet another, until one would rush from the room. Eventually a plump Mamason would emerge and order them all out immediately, and big burly Frenchmen would descend from heaven. And nothing else would happen. Nothing else would ever happen, per se.

Nobody wondered who she was. A couple of them — lacking discipline — started to, but they caught themselves. Better never to see a name or face — either would suffer loss of dignity: dignity was the last to leave, a bumbling guest that overstayed, desperately trying to find more subjects to discuss, finding excuses to stall, harming herself on accident. What followed was horror, something worse than death itself.

She was instantly forgotten.

Or nearly. The girl that found her recoiled in horror many nights. She never forgot the smell — it seemed to infect her thoughts and dreams — a darkness that licked her and raped her in the night. The look of the decaying skin, but was it skin anymore? It was nothing but rotten tissue, clinging to a corpse like she clung to life itself. She wandered, as always, around and around, and accidentally made eye contact with the Dead. Habit. She stared blankly, not quite comprehending from spiritual exhaustion, blasé, but perhaps it was better than not working enough, and…

"I am taking you out of here."

"Oh?"

She added sarcastically.

"I'm not interested."

He shrugged.

"It is not exactly your choice."
He smiled maliciously.
A chill went down her spine.
She rushed from the room.

CHAPTER 11

From the gloom Mamason materialized and swatted her viciously.

She smashed against the wall and fell down, naked and ashamed.

Beaten. Again.

"Get back out there."

Mamason growled menacingly. Her jowls quivered as if she were waiting to bite her head off.

She cooly turned around and went back out. Out where? Anywhere else. Inside she whimpered like a tiny, wet, abandoned puppy on a cold and wintery night. But she was grotesque, lacking all the cuteness of innocence. A ghost of a soul.

He laughed.

"Back so soon?"

The feeling of having no choice.

The worst part of this life.

Or was it the feeling of having no hope? No future?

She had never succeeded at harakiri.

She was too weak.

He stuck out his arm.

She took it elegantly.

"You have a new life now."

"Shut up."

She cursed him.

Darkness. They walked through the gloom. Slowly. The doors all opened, and the agonizing night received them.

He paused.

"I prefer the night."

"Oh?"

"It is the time to think."

"Mm."

"The only time to really think."

"Really."

She felt contempt.

CHAPTER 12

"I want nothing."

"Oh?"

She laughed without humor.

"You are free."

"I never wanted to be free."

"You have no choice."

The sound of freedom.

"I am going back."

"You know you can never leave."

She paused.

"What happened to freedom?"

Sarcasm.

He patted her head.

"An illusion."

"But a pleasant one." He added, as he searched for the moon in the sky. If he could only see the moon, he would know what to say.

CHAPTER 13

"I cannot stay. I have nothing with me."

She tried.

He shrugged.

"We will shop tomorrow."

He indicated her bag.

"You have enough for tonight."

She rolled her eyes.

"I thought I was not working."

"Work is God's plan."

"I thought it was God's curse."

He smiled, and she noticed suddenly how pleasant she felt.

"That too."

CHAPTER 14

It was a lavish apartment, with more rooms than she had ever imagined any place could have. She could not help the awe that manifested on her haggard features.

He watched her expression with satisfaction.

"You will like it here."

She frowned.

"You are the devil." She returned bitterly. "You think you can buy that which has no price."

He waved off the words, but suddenly grew serious.

"You want to go back?"

"Yes."

"Why?"

"I hate you."

"You have a problem."

"I know."

"You are too beautiful for this life."

"Are you finally ready?"

"You really are free."

"You are wasting my time."

He again waved a hand.

"You need not worry."

She grew silent.

"Was it something I said?"

"No."

"You lost the mood?"

She approached.

He pulled back, and walked out, but as he disappeared into the next room, he called out.

"Follow me."

CHAPTER 15

What was most astounding about the apartment was the light. She had never been in a well-lit place. How vibrant everything looked ! She needed to remember this place in her mind. Finally Mamason would be pleased. Overnights were becoming rare for her, and she was beaten more and more often. She could not wait to see the curiosity on her boss's face, proof she finally had something her boss wanted.

She stopped.

Who was this man? She tried and tried to place him, but she could not remember him, and she always remembered guests. Or at least their faces. His was too new, too fresh, and too arrogant. He did not belong, and her instincts screamed every sort of warning imaginable.

What could she do? Of course he was right: she had no choice. If he raped her... that was her job. When had she not been raped? If he killed her, he killed her; she had been ready to die for a long time. But it was not death that scared her, but something far more horrifying: his veracity. It was nothing she had the courage to consider. Tonight she would do her job, and tomorrow back to work.

Why was he so evasive?

What if he passed on a bad report?

She shivered.

"Please." She caught his sleeve. "Let me take care of you. What's wrong?"

She grew desperate.

"I will not report you. Calm down."

"I do not believe you."

"Please."

He stopped in front of a door.

"This is your room."

"Let me stay with you."

"No."

"I cannot be alone."

"No."

"I really cannot be alone."

She fought down panic.

Bona fide earnest.

He paused. Perhaps she really had never slept alone. Perhaps she really did have fear. Fear of what? Being alone? Or something else?

"I will show you my room."

They walked.

He paused in front of another door.

"I will be in here."

She grabbed his arm.

"I will stay with you."

"No."

"Why?"

She felt hurt and confused. He was not behaving quite

like anybody she had met. Her clients fell into categories that she could instantly detect. Who was he?

"I sleep alone."

"Why am I here?"

Exasperation.

He shrugged.

"I am scared. I will leave now."

"I expect you at 8 o'clock in the morning for breakfast."

She sighed. She knew they never could have left unless he had already paid. What did he pay? What was she going for?

He read her mind.

"Mamason is quite happy, I can assure you."

She felt bitter. The answer was worse than the question.

Where did his authority come from?

Money was everything in this life.

They walked back to her room, where he pointed at a button by her bed.

"If you hit this, a butler will attend to you."

Her eyes widened. That sounded even more terrifying.

"What about you?"

"I will knock precisely at 8 o'clock. Please be ready for breakfast."

He gestured.

"The bathroom is there. Everything you need is here. Everything here is yours."

She looked around. He was not wrong. The room was a large apartment unto itself, larger than any bedroom she had ever seen, with floor to ceiling windows overlooking the city.

She gasped as she noticed the view for the first time.

She had never been so high.

Exhilaration.

She tried to hide her emotion.

He waited politely, discreetly pretending not to notice, but looking quite smug.

She hated him, but she was suddenly thankful she did not have to work.

A night to herself in her own apartment.

A dream.

But what terror awaited her there?

Yet she still tried one more time. She sat on the bed and assumed her most winning pose. If she could have him, she knew she would be able to break him. She would be able to figure him out. It only needed the right timing, the right setting.

"Come sit here." With a smooth and sultry voice, she indicated the space by her.

A scene of perfect practice.

He smiled genially.

"Good night."

He disappeared.

The door closed. She rushed over and bolted it.

Hypnotized, she drifted back to the windows overlooking the city.

Was this her city?

How could you tell from up here?

CHAPTER 9.65

The doctor somberly approached.

"We really are not sure... We are forced to advise... "

His voice lowered, and the man's eyes bulged as the words absorbed.

She suddenly screamed in agony, baptized in her own blood, knifing through reflection.

He woke up every night to her shrieks.

The sheets were wet.

Was it his sweat?

Or her blood?

He would rather have had her. He could never forgive her, and he could never forgive him.

They ruined his life. They destroyed him.

And they were supposed to love him.

CHAPTER 9.66

Why did she do it?

CHAPTER 9.89

He had no origin story.

His dad hated him.

He never knew he had a mother, until one day in school a teacher told the class everybody has a mother.

He was shocked.

That was the day he knew he was different. He could never be like the other kids. He ran out of the room screaming.

He was 10.

CHAPTER 16

8 o'clock came early.

He knocked, expecting nothing.

She answered the door, and he led her through several rooms to an ornate baroque room. Every ounce of the room was decorated, and the ceiling had elaborate paintings of Renaissance musicians. Rich wood shelves full of ancient texts lined the walls, and the floor matched. Two majestic chairs faced each other over a carved wood table, whose legs and edges were carefully sculpted with floral designs.

They sat and were immediately attended to.

"Tea? Coffee?"

"Milk?" she replied.

"Milk it is. Coffee for me."

The waiter turned and left.

"And make it fresh milk."

He called out after him.

"Naturally, sir."

A man with a giant mustache in a towering toque approached.

"Ahhhhh Bernard!"

"Morning, sir."

He bowed.

The host turned to his guest.

"What would you like?"

She paused, unsure of herself, and he intuited her thoughts.

"Oh, you can ask for anything. No worries."

"Well," She hesitated, wondering how far she could take this. "I've always wanted caviar."

"Perfect!" Bernard exclaimed. "Someone with taste!"

"What else?" The host pressed.

She trembled inside.

She felt strangely aroused.

What was happening?

CHAPTER 9.91

He cheerfully walked the streets of town, dreaming of the one he loved.

The most peculiar advertisement.

WANTED: GRAVE WATCHER

What a Fate for the young, morbid, unemployed man !

A most curious interview.

An older distinguished gentleman.

"How do you feel about the dead?"

"The most important sign of a civilization is how it looks after its dead. How a person he remembers the past and cultivates it: that is his whole character."

The gentleman sat in silence for a long time, studying the boy.

The boy fidgeted.

He slowly prepared a cigar, lit it, took a long puff, and passed it to the boy.

The boy shook his head.

"Sorry, sir. My parents would never approve."

He bowed deeply.

"We must smoke together." The man replied earnestly.

The boy hesitated.

"Whisky, or cognac?"

"Whisky I suppose."

The boy spoke deferentially.

CHAPTER 9.92

The man lit his cigar and handed it to the boy. He took a long draw on his own, realizing the boy needed an example. The latter watched intently. Exactly how he breathed in and out, how the instrument protruded slightly to the left, how he held it in his fingers. He replicated it exactly. He coughed 10 times, for the 10 Commandments.

But he had never learned them.

"You need to know about this woman."

The man continued.

He paused, and a tear rolled down his left eye. Then one from his right eye. And another from his left. His free hand dabbed his upper cheek with a handkerchief.

The boy sat very still, because there was nothing as sacred as tears. There was no greater meaning in this life.

"I met her in school. She was one of very few women who studied at the university in those days...

"I saw her in the back of class, and I was struck by her artistry....

"I never talked to girls in those days. I had a strict upbringing... it felt wrong to even look at a woman...

"But somehow... I guess Fate designed it all...

"I saw her in the lobby of the School, and I said hello...

"Rather than walking onward, she stopped, and looked at me, and we talked... !"

The man grew flushed with excitement as he remembered. A light shone on his face, and his features conformed to the optimism of love. Another paroxysm of suffering. His head fell into his arms. Weeping. He cried out.

The boy ached, but he dare not move. Like all boys, he desperately wanted to move around, but he had old-fashioned respect. The kind nobody else his age understood. He was alone.

He gradually lifted his head, and stared into the vastness.

"It was a normal conversation... she told me where she was from... how she had changed the last few years... how she had branched out, like an olive tree, like a cherry blossom in the spring...

"She was a blossom. Nothing has ever been more alive....

"Even when she fled.... she wanted that baby... more than anything... more than me..."

He howled in pain.

"I never forgave her. I was jealous! Forgive me!" He cried out. "Forgive me, Mujaki !!!!!" He screamed toward the heavens, not quite believing she heard him, but trying to reach her in spite of his doubts. He clasped his fists, and they shook with the tremendous energy that he pressed them together with. His whole body trembled. He hammered the table, and beat his brow several times.

The boy decided to take a sip of his whisky. He did it very slowly as not to draw attention. The man was not really speaking with him — to himself, to his wife, to his Fate ....

who knew? The whisky burned, but he decided he liked it. It felt nice to be burned a little — not too much, but a little.

"I did not want the child, but she did... and I lost control...

The man grew suddenly dark and angry.

"She....

He shook his head, as if to clear all that was wrong with the world.

"I was so insistent.... she left, and she had to...

"We never spoke again....

There was a long pause, and he settled down, and took another deep draw, blowing it right in the boys face. His eyes closed, but he tried not to cough. He held his breath.

"But I found out who her doctor was, and I was there... I showed up when....

He choked.

"When she passed, I was there!!!! She never knew, but I was there!!! Maybe she knew??? I don't know, I don't know.... I just don't know....

"I never left her!!!!"

He cried out indignantly.

"I never did. I was always there!"

He spoke as one trying to convince somebody. Himself?

"The decision...

"I had the boy....

"She was gone...."

He buried his head and wept and wept and wept and wept.

The boy finished his glass, and left without another word.

CHAPTER 9.93

He stopped at a flower shop.

"Greetings, Sonkei ! Your flowers are in the usual place."

She indicated a small table on the side of the room, apart from the other flower displays.

The boy bowed. "How is the family?"

"Well ! Yours?"

The boy bowed. "Well also."

They locked eyes. They felt the love of two people who shared something. He had never known anybody so beautiful, but he was too scared to tell her. Would they miss it? Would they miss the glory of young and innocent love?

They had no idea what, but they knew they felt something together.

Something deep.

Something about life.

CHAPTER 9.95

The boy continued on, and finally reached the gate to the cemetery.

He unlocked it, continued through, and carefully closed the gate behind him. He knew the path without watching, the path to Muzaki's grave. He was lost in thoughts of the girl who gave him the flowers. If only... If only....

Suddenly he froze.

He was here.

CHAPTER 9.96

FUJII MUJAKI

1977-2002

A beautiful stone.

He was slowly pouring water on it.

The water trickled down.

When it reached the cracked soil, it disappeared, as if it never were at all.

He set down the pitcher, and took a step back, to survey the scene.

He stood so still that from afar it seemed he was fixed like a different sort of stone.

He waited patiently.

Death, come quickly.

CHAPTER 9.98

The boy solemnly approached with both bouquets.

    Nobody said a word. Neither acknowledged the other.

    He left, carrying yesterday's flowers out with him.

    The stone radiated in youthful beauty: the right side adorned with spider lilies, the left overflowing with yellow and red tulips.

    The man went through every memory, but there were fewer and fewer to go through. He desperately tried to remember more of their first conversation, but she was always the one who knew. They always worked through their memories together. Without her, it all faded... it...

    They would both remember bits and pieces, and together they built the picture, each time... was it the same as before? Perhaps the memories evolved with them. Perhaps they remembered differently depending on what they felt, on what they needed.

    Now the picture was fading.... The flowers fresh every-day, but the memories rotting away... He felt the loss. Every day he felt the loss. He could see little else in life. No other family, no other friends, not even himself. He missed everything now. Since she was gone, he had missed it all, all the joy and happiness of life.

Losing her was hard, but losing the memories of her was far worse.

He sighed.

It was time to bring his son.

What did his son even know?

Nothing.

Did he suspect he had killed his wife?

Did he ever have an inkling?

Was it possible to have a memory that one never lived?

Implanted memories, inherited memories, passed down memories... were all truer than lived ones.

CHAPTER -7.5

Thus began the most beautiful time in both of their lives.

They traveled the world.

Inyoku was enamored with every experience.

She clung to him in every way, in every single way.

He adored her for the respect and admiration she showed him.

She praised him.

She complimented him.

And she meant every word.

They both had everything they ever wanted, and all the bliss that life could offer.

But Kotan never dared to fully enjoy himself. Somehow he felt it was wrong to feel happiness. He knew he did not deserve it, and he suspected the happier he was now, the more he would have to suffer later. Sorrow always balanced joy — it was Fate.

Always he feared the coming sorrow.

Always.

It was a matter of time.

CHAPTER 17

Italy.

Inner Mongolia.

Japan.

Zanzibar.

Dubai.

Cape Town.

Amsterdam.

Timbuktu.

Santiago.

So much passion.

So much love.

How many beds had they enjoyed? How many baths? How many moments cuddled together in the most intimate ways?

How many scenes of nature?

How many Mountains? Oceans? Waterfalls?

City views?

They had their own code, their own way of speaking. They could hold entire conversations based only on travel references... on shared experiences... Finish each other's sentences... Know every exclamation... every imprecation... all their quirks... all the ways they saw the world....

CHAPTER -10.6

He noticed a couple in the rain, zig-zagging through the parking lot, hopping to avoid puddles, pointing out the dangers of the deep puddles to each other.

Watch that spot.

Watch it !

Pointing there.

And over there. That one.

He felt very touched, watching love in action, having none and knowing there would never be any for him.

He was glad somebody still loved somebody else.

He was glad there was a little bit of warmth in the world.

Who knows whether he would ever see anything so adorable again?

He could not decide if he loved his memories, or hated them. Most of the time they felt like torture. They showed what he might have had; if things had gone differently, what he would have had. They reminded him what he had lost, what evil had taken away, what was now a void. Was it evil? Or was it simply the way she was made? The way it was Fated to be?

For a moment he pictured her the way she used to be. He saw her next to him on the balcony in the morning in her sheen. The gentle clink of the porcelain being placed back on porcelain. They gazed into the future — blissfully unaware of its darkness. They saw only the morning Sunshine burning through morning Mist. The world opened up, the birds twittered excitedly, the gentle eucalyptus and pandan swirled about them, in their life of dreams. For a moment he fell in love again. Was it with her? Or was it with the thought of happiness? Falling in love with a memory was pathetic, scarcely better than a girlfriend in the clouds, one that never existed at all, one that came from nothing, one that never lived. One that never spoke from emotion, one that never acted impulsively, one that never knew the fire of true passion. At least his had happened — he believed — if memories could be trusted.

But they never could: no more than dreams, no more than the riches at the end of the rainbow, no more than those that he loved with all his heart. Perhaps that is all they were.

Dreams.

CHAPTER 10.37

Kotan was listening to an elderly man when a beatific young woman floated in. He tried very hard to pay attention to his conversant, but instead he tracked her every move. She caught him. He blushed, but he was no match. She possessed the steal of arrogance born from the accurate assumption that everybody watched her. Her life — her game — a self-glorifying quest to humiliate all who struggled to control their eyes. She was never ignored, and she knew it.

Kotan felt deeply ashamed, and, self-aware, decided to thoroughly ignore her.

Old people are never noticed, and they know it. Yet Kotan gave him his undivided attention. He felt moral for the first time in weeks, as he turned from her pleasure to his suffering. She could wait.

Equity of attention.

Perhaps Equity was not all about money.

CHAPTER 10.62

He wondered why his principal was there.

Put his ear to the ground.

"Not having a mother... hard on him..."

He nodded gravely.

They bowed.

"Let me know if there is anything else we can do...."

They bowed.

"You are most kind...."

"... ... He does have a counselor... I assure you this will not happen again... I apologize...."

He bowed deeply.

"I understand...."

He bowed.

"I hate to intrude...."

"Not at all...."

"Good day to you."

"Good day, Yoshida-sama."

"Let me show you out...."

"Thank you."

"Oh... before.... I forget...

"and do let me know about the club needs…"

He bowed.

"Of course, dear friend. Farewell, Yufuku-san…"

They bowed.

Kotan rushed out from hiding.

"Father, why was Yoshida-sama here???"

He patted his son on the head.

His eyes glistened.

The greatest joy of a father. Covering for his children.

Taking away a little of life's suffering.

For a season.

It could never last, but this time, this time he would help him out.

The tears?

The tears were because his son would never know.

Somewhere deep inside, a form of purity lingered, and it surprised him and frightened him. It was the only time he had done something for his son. He could never love his son, but he would at least have the advantages of Wealth.

CHAPTER 11.4

She had the youthful habit of entertainment obsession... Or rather the youthful habit of not knowing it was wise to hide one's entertainment obsession...

"... So what kind of movies do you like?"

Kotan shrugged.

"What kind of music do you listen to?

"I never listen to music."

"What shows do you watch?"

"I never watch shows."

With each question she became more and more incredulous, more and more stunned.

"You are joking."

She thought he was.

He was not.

He never joked.

Maybe he would have learned how if he watched shows.

She was self-aware enough to know that entertainment was destroying her. On the outside she good-naturedly mocked him. On the inside she admired him.

He sensed it, and began to fall in love.
All he ever wanted was to be admired by someone.

CHAPTER 11.42

Inyoku practiced the art of disassociation. Time after time after time... day after night after night after night after day after night.... forming no connections.... no bonds... yet convincingly attaching to her regulars... but not really... business... there was something... but to feel something was to feel pain. She shook it off, and turned to her phone — her one solace in life. Entertainment offered an escape, a way to distract herself whenever she felt tempted to connect with the world. Like all great Deceivers, it was the opposite of what it promised. Because it never really consoled her. It never worked. She escaped nothing. Nor would she forever.

But tonight, before she passed out, she dared to dream. She tried to imagine the world out there somewhere. She tried to imagine what happiness was. How happy people felt. Somewhere deep in her past she saw images of a playground, of other children running, and playing tag, and throwing balls, and laughing and squealing and crying. How long since she had seen a child?

Tonight she felt overwhelmed by Desire. She longed for one of her own, but that was impossible. She longed to love someone, but she never could. There was nobody to love. Her own child, and only her own child, could be trusted — an innocent, crying baby could always be trusted. For the first time, she could love somebody.

She wondered at the possibility of love. At how that would feel, to hold her own baby, to look into her baby's eyes. She decided she wanted a daughter, a beautiful little girl with her own blond hair and grey-blue eyes, with a beauty mark slightly northeast of her lips, and a lovely dimple on the other side. Ears a little too small, and a chin a little bit too pointed. But that was later — for now her face was fat and round and healthy and rosy. Her cry was fragile, and soft, and adorable. Everything about her was perfect.

But a baby needed a father.

She sighed.

She fell asleep in deep despair.

Even her dreams were dark and troubled.

When she awoke, her pillow was wet.

Not from sweat.

From tears.

CHAPTER 18

It was his last day.

Rather than looking ahead, he looked to the past. He wistfully watched the people he worked with. For the first time he considered what they meant to him. Suddenly he appreciated them in a new way, but only as he was leaving them.

Forever.

He remembered the old poem.

"One has to leave
before one understands
What one has left..."

Would he see them again?

A couple of them said goodbye. His favorite workmate told him she would miss him, and he felt so moved that he dared not look at her, for fear of weeping. They wished each other good luck, and they meant it.

When he passed through the doors at the end of the day, he felt mostly confusion. How was he supposed to feel? He was going through the doors to a new life, but it felt and looked the same as any other day he walked out....

Hundreds of times... Thousands? He was captive to his senses. It was impossible to understand the change he was facing, because he could not see it, could not feel it, could not even hear about it.

He would rather not look ahead — he was terrified of the unknown. When he looked back, he felt depressed: lost years... the waste... the failure... the utter ruin of his life. He tried to concentrate on the present, but his head hurt, and he saw purple.

He needed to lose himself in something.

He needed to die.

CHAPTER 12.1

She nodded in the direction of the door.

"Pretty crazy that he actually worked here, huh?"

"What do you mean?"

She stared at him incredulously.

"You mean... wait ! You mean you never knew????"

Confusion.

"Knew what?"

"Kotan's dad is a trillionaire or something."

Baffled. "You're joking... Kotan??"

She whistled. "Wowwwwwww."

CHAPTER 12.2

Two dogs approached each other.
    One wagged her head disapprovingly.
    "Gertrude, you've put on a few."
    She hung her head.
    "I've been sneaking biscuits." She confessed.
    Her tail sunk between her legs.

CHAPTER 12.3

Kotan asked her to marry him.
    She was shocked.
    She immediately said yes.
    It would be foolish not to.
    He had money.

CHAPTER 12.75

"I see steak, and I just lose it." He confessed.

"It's okay, George. It took me years to say no to a steak."

"It's really those treats that do it, anyway." Festus added. "Steak is healthy. Keto…"

"I beg and beg for treats." George pawed the ground. "I gotta exercise more…."

CHAPTER 19

Kotan decided to teach. What better way to make an impact than with day to day interaction? He would be a good influence; he would make a difference in young lives, during the most impressionable time in life, a lasting legacy. If he could impart a morsel of wisdom, he would finally have a place in this world.

But the students lied to him.

They were cruel.

They showed no respect.

He quickly became disillusioned. There was no hope after all. Nobody could make a difference there. School was a twisted sort of prison, where the only way to survive was to develop an aggressive apathy toward all things. If he were going to be apathetic, he should at least earn lots of money.

He quit.

He was wrong about everything.

How many times did he have to start over?

Each time grew harder.

And he was older now.

He no longer wanted to try.
He could not work that hard anymore.

CHAPTERS 19.01 – 2110.88

Kotan was living in poverty. He could not afford an apartment, but by some miracle he had an old car, so he slept in it. Soon this would fail him, and he would locate a luxurious spot under a bridge. The world was closing in, suffocating him. The pressure grew, and he strained to see, tried to listen, tried to feel. When he considered his situation, a claustrophobic wave poured over him. He grew worse and worse, emaciated, outside and in.

He knew he had already died.

The rest of life was waiting for others to realize it.

He saw no way out, no hope and no future. He knew money — he was cursed to know money. The knowledge was in his blood, so he could never get rid of it, not without leeches, or needles. Better to work and never think; better to shut off cognition, but he was cursed with a mind that worked ceaselessly, tormenting him with a reality both miserable and oppressive. He could not distract himself like others. He could not entertain himself with mind-dumbing yarns about heroes that would save him. Nor with images of copulation, to imagine it was his own member, to create a pointless simulation. Imagination was evil — it was why he was doomed to this mess in the first place, yearning for something that never existed, nor could ever exist.

He understood the number he needed to survive, and he understood that number was impossible to reach. There was no use in trying for the impossible, for pressing toward an invisible mark, one that always moved farther and farther away. To walk forward was to walk backwards, and to walk backwards was to walk into darkness. The old days were gone — the optimism had dried up along with the opportunity. One could never rise from the ashes — there was no Dark Knight. Just a bunch of people in pit, waiting, waiting for death. There was nothing else to wait for.

Someday they would see him under the bridge; someday they would realize he was dead, they day he began to stink. Then somebody would take his body somewhere and convert it to ash. But in the meantime they would walk around him and pretend he was never there. It was easier that way, easier for everybody.

CHAPTER 20

By some miracle, a little girl ran up to him to hug him. He turned away coldly, but not without cursing the System.

That was illegal.

Both things.

CHAPTER 21

"Customer 42, your order is ready."

CHAPTER 22

Kotan walked through the cemetery.

Jimmy Coygney
    1899-1931
    "He plugged the wrong man."

Freddie Austraire
    1899-1935
    "He never should have f— that llama."

He raised his eyebrows.

CHAPTER 23

Frankie Clark
1950-2021
"Should have gotten vaccinated."

Lucille Clark
1953-2021
"Should NOT have gotten vaccinated."

Kotan nodded grimly.

CHAPTER 24

Katie Hepbarn
    1907-1951
    "Should have learned to say NO."

CHAPTER 25

Kotan looked glumly at the other line. They were moving quickly, faces full of hope, beaming with anticipation.

His own line was frozen. People in the back were shouting obscenities. A few were shoving other people aside. One guy pulled out a gun and started shooting it in the air. Three women were graphically —. A young boy was screaming.

He always chose the wrong line.

CHAPTER 21.5

He reached the stop sign nearly simultaneously with two other drivers at the intersection. One never knew exactly what would happen in these scenarios.

One of the drivers was a beautiful 24 year-old young lady, and he felt a jolt of excitement when they made eye contact. It all disappeared when she motioned him through, and rapidly pivoted to motion the other driver through. She used both hands like a practiced traffic cop. He was not impressed. He instantly lost all attraction for her.

Traffic cops never made good wives.

CHAPTER 26

They were from the same litter.

"Fred, you're walking kind of funny. What's going on?" Bernie asked.

Fred hung his head.

"Stephen had me fixed."

"Oh, I'm sorry Fred."

Bernie took a paw and patted his head.

CHAPTER 27

The life of a teacher.

One boy started snickering.

What caused him to laugh?

An indistinguishable sound.

More laughter.

A phone rings.

Giggling.

The life of a teacher.

Darkness.

He looked out the window and saw a dark world of ash.

He was forgetting what the Shire looked like.

CHAPTER 27.00777777

"Kotan, you're not really worth that much."

She shook her head grimly.

"It is over."

Kotan nodded.

"And how much are you worth?"

She paused thoughtfully.

"Probably five times that much."

Kotan shot her.

She coughed up blood, and gave up the ghost.

"And how much are you worth now?"

He asked politely.

He waited patiently.

"Never mind." he added. "It was rhetorical question."

He bowed and took his leave.

It was over.

CHAPTER 27.07

For days Kotan went over all the reasons he may have been fired. He could think of nothing he did wrong. He could think of nothing he could have improved. He was a perfect employee.

CHAPTER 27.08

Kotan attended the funeral. He appeared thoughtful during the service. Her surviving wife was disconsolate. He felt sorry for her, while acknowledging she made a horrific choice. Mother was there too. He introduced himself and gave his deepest condolences.

It was unfortunate she had to die. He counted her as a dear friend, and though she betrayed him, he still held great affection for her.

CHAPTER 27.09

On the way back to work, he dropped by his estate attorney's office.

Mother would be taken care of.

CHAPTER 27.1

Kotan could never sit at airports. He paced and paced, lost in profound thought, so deep and troubling that he was aware of nothing. He always felt a vague restlessness haunting him. Robbing his peace.

He walked through the entire terminal 20 times.

At some point he woke up and realized he was walking the wrong way on a moving walkway.

He was walking, but not moving forward.

He had two choices. He could press on still faster. Or he could stop, and let the walkway and the laws of decency have their way, and carry him back to where he began.

He solemnly chose the latter.

Fate always tugged him back to where he began.

A kite in the wind.

CHAPTER 27.2

He tried to shove the food cart through, but a fat man spilled into the aisle. The man was kind, but he was too fat. He asked a kindly elderly lady to put her tray up, but she would not. He felt a hand pat him on his backside as he passed. Another vicious passenger objects vociferously to being called "ma'am." The turbulence suddenly launches him into a sleeping passenger, who shouts imprecations, red-faced — a raging alcoholic. His credit card machine quits. Again. He stands there, waiting, and absorbs the murmurs of impatience. He feels perpetually lonely and tired.

Finally he decides to quit. He moves to Hawaii, because in his imagination he loves Hawaii. But he hates it there. He could never get ahead of his discontentment.

CHAPTER 27.3

Kotan's biggest fear was forgetting the past. He hoped he died before he ever fell into dementia. Once he lost touch with the past, the past was worthless; the whole of life was worthless. Dementia probably would happen, but the biggest sin was to forget.

Kotan often passed by his elementary school. He tried to remember. Each time it grew fuzzier. He could recall almost nothing. He was gradually losing his humanity. Now only a couple names surfaced in his mind — the rest were forgotten, those he had promised he would never forget, those that he knew would never be forgotten... all were lost.

He was wrong.

The only names he never forgot were the names of his crushes, and he would carry the burden of those to the grave, the sorrow and restlessness — what might have been — with all of them. He told himself he regretted nothing, but he never believed himself, and he would never stop wondering.

CHAPTER 28

It was a normal day. Kotan went out to check his mailbox, mostly to see if a federal agency was bullying him again. Often there was a loan or credit card offer to deal with. Sometimes a political advertisement.

Today Kotan received the surprise of his life. It looked like a personal letter. The address was written by hand, and he recognized the sender as an old friend. It *was* a personal letter.

He was stunned.

He almost passed out. Steadied himself on a wall. Tremblingly he managed to tear the top open with a finger.

What was going on?

He slowly removed the letter from the envelope. He was in a fog. His eyesight was blurry, and he struggled to focus. He shook like a wet dog. It was too much.

He slid the letter back in the envelope.

He would read it later.

When he was ready.

CHAPTER 28.555555

His father appeared.

"Kotan."

"Yes."

"In all my travels I've learned one thing. Everybody is out to get you. Everybody wants something from you. Anything and everything they can get. And they do not care how they get it."

He paused.

"You can never be too careful."

The boy listened intently, and with great wonder.

His father never told him anything.

CHAPTER 29

Kotan again determined his wife was cheating. The first few times, he diligently tracked and sleuthed, but this time required no effort. She behaved the same each time: a little too restless; a little too happy; a little too kind.

The stuff guilt was made of.

It was up to him whether to ignore it or continue on in some kind of nightmarish fraud of a marriage.

It was remarkable the extent to which she could not care about her husband.

He never ceased to marvel, because he never ceased to not understand.

Years of fond memories.

Travels.

Laughter.

Intimate moments.

It had to mean something.

It had to.

CHAPTER 747.66

Kotan wanted to die. He did not want to outlive all of his friends, because he was selfish: dying first would spare him the sorrow of all those funerals. Was it really better to be the one that lives? That grows old, that has nobody left to spend that precious time over coffee with? What good was travel or writing or music or art if nobody knew you anymore? What good was travel if you had nobody to visit? The land did not speak to you in the same way as a person, neither strangers the same as friends.

The tiniest sliver of guilt caused his only reservation, guilt from the thought of dying before his father, something not even his miserable, cruel father deserved.

He would wait his turn.

CHAPTER 30

Wait!

One more passenger sprinted toward the gate, waving his arms and screaming for mercy. He barreled through the causeway, fueled with tenacity caused by utter desperation.

His mother was dying in Tel Aviv.

The flight attendant stamped her feet impatiently, but she kept the door open.

When the man climbed aboard, silence met him.

Judgement.

A beautiful woman appeared and strolled in as the door was closing. The attendant huffed, but dutifully held it open.

She stepped on the plane, and the attendant announced the final passenger was aboard.

Huzzahs from the back.

The plane finally started moving.

Raucous cheers from the gallery.

Wait!

Somebody has a phobia of seat belts.

Another delay.

The gallery holds its breath.

Trembling, sweating... slowly... ever so slowly... he lines up the sides...

Shaking too much...

At last...

Lined up.

Everybody hears the click.

The plane erupts with applause.

The man smiles through tears.

He has never achieved anything in his life until now.

Wait !

The flight attendant is struggling with a bag.

Pushing. Shoving.

Grunting.

Time turns to molasses.

The plane grows eerily silent.

Hope fades.

Finally an irritable fat man unbuckles and approaches.

Several attempts.

Failure.

Failure.

The galley groans.

They dare not look.

Failure.

On the count of three.

Together.

In perfect symmetry, they throw themselves at it with the whole of their force, with their last liter of courage.

The gallery dared not hope.

The bag slides into place.

Eruption. Desperate applause.

The couple embraces. Tears everywhere. The two feel

entwined forever. The man's face, flushed with exhaustion, beaming like Moses. The woman holds him far longer than the usual hug requires.

They wish the moment could last forever.

This moment, the most beautiful of their lives.

CHAPTER 31.1

He never suspected it would be his last moment of happiness. Nor had he even recognized he had been happy until much later, after he grew quite morose again. It was then he realized — in the dark of night, as he sipped his cognac and gazed at stars far above — that the times he believed were sad... how happy he was!

He had never recognized what he experienced in life, nor had he ever fully understood any of it. He decided it was only the moments that never happened that could be fully understood.

Only dreams.

He sighed.

The happiest moments made the saddest memories.

CHAPTER 31.2

The two married and had 12 children. Finally she died of a stroke, and in the coffin her face looked the same as it did that day in the plane. He saw the same flushed excitement, and his soul leapt within him. There was a moment, just a moment, when...

Soon after he himself died. Did it matter how? Except it was in the most romantic way possible — from love that could never be rekindled, from a love forever lost. And without love... what was life? What was life without her love? Those that knew them briefly remembered the love they had toward each other, the beauty of their mutual admiration, the endless possibility of their shared dreams, and the pinnacle of life's fulfillment in their unwavering mutual support. Through their entire miserable lives, their love endured, and burned brighter each day.

Their legend gave wonder for awhile to a jaded generation that never witnessed love, a love that would never return the same way. When it came back, it would be without the deliberate and intentional innocence necessary to sustain it. The younger ones were alone, or sometimes together, but they could never understand how to give or how to receive such a gift.

The furnace went out.

The secret of the fire was lost.

The term — so much as it was understood — the term that used to drive the world, was mercilessly mocked.

Over cognac two lovers sat, sharing a moment, at a most pleasant and cozy jazz club on the 34th floor, in the bowels of the bustling city, looking for what they were running from.

A place dreams came to die, and where love could never be.

They thought they found something.

But soon they felt lonely again.

CHAPTER 31.25

Trying to shove food cart through... but the man is spilling into the aisle...

Trying to get man to put tray up, but he will not.

Another man touches her hinder parts as she glides by.

What can she do?

Someday the right member would enter, and she would feel ecstasy and bliss for the first and last time.

She waited.

Deep down she knew it would never happen.

She knew what seemed like pleasure never really was.

She was too wise for this world.

Yet somehow it never stopped her from trying.

She tried and tried and tried.

A moment here. A moment there.

How many ways were there to measure life?

There was pleasure. The only virtue was pleasure.

The only life was temporary, one that would be gone in the morning, one that never stuck, and the whole of one's life passed the same way as a night scented with eucalyptus and littered with the soft rush of satin, the softest fur slippers, and the most beautiful view of the sea.

Inyoku sighed.

The way of death.

CHAPTER 48.001

He was ready.

It was time to read the letter.

His breath started coming from his throat, thinly, rapidly. His heart pounded; he felt the pulse of it behind his ears; his head swelled. He was becoming a monster. He pictured himself with horns.

He mopped his suddenly moist forehead with a forearm. He held the envelope a long time, still wondering if it were too precious to read. Would he die? Slowly, with tremendous care, he coaxed it out of the envelope into his clammy palm.

With his other hand, he unstuck it, and gently found the corner with a thumb and began to separate the two sides.

The front!

The card itself was white, but the front was a deep blue.

His favorite color.

He paused.

The letters were artistic and flowery.

He loved art.

He loved flowers.
Two simple words.
Thank you.

CHAPTER 48.111

It was time.

Kotan finally began in earnest to part the two legs of the card.

He tried not to peak as the card began to open.

But he could not help it.

He could see a lot of writing.

More than he expected.

Suddenly he froze.

He began to panic.

It was too much.

He quickly put it the letter back in the envelope, and carefully sealed it.

When he was ready.

CHAPTER 48.749

All day he paced around, like a polar bear at the zoo.

But he felt more like a sand cat.

More nervous.

More careful.

Much smaller.

He questioned everything.

He wondered about his life.

What was he doing?

How did it come to this?

How had his friend thought of him?

Why did his friend send him a card?

He simply could not figure it out.

He could figure nothing out.

He did not understand.

He did not understand.

He had never received affection from anybody in his life.

Even his wife was an unfaithful whore.

He did not deserve this.

He did not know what to do.

He did not understand.

What was he supposed to feel?

How was he supposed to react?

It was all so new.

It was all so stressful.

Exciting…. but mostly stressful.

Deep down he felt more honor than he had ever felt.

But he was reluctant to accept it.

He paced.

And he paced.

And he paced.

He did not understand.

He did not understand.

He could not understand.

Hours went by.

Day turned to night.

Night turned to day.

At some point he passed out again.

CHAPTER 48.75

Kotan woke up two days later, thirsty, and nearly dead.

He grunted.

Life was suffering.

CHAPTER 49

He managed to drag himself over to where the envelope had fallen.

He slowly — ever so slowly — secured it with his stiff and useless fingers.

But again his consciousness slipped away.

CHAPTER 49.9

It was dark.

He was dying.

He saw unpleasant visions. People yelling at him. Kicking him. Hatred. A lifetime of suffering.

They were not visions.

They were memories.

CHAPTER 50

But this card. This card was something different.

He opened his eyes.

CHAPTER 51

Weeks later.

Another try.

He took the card in his hand.

But he shuddered uncontrollably, and the card fell to the earth.

Slowly he bent down.

He could not retrieve it.

He sat down nearby and watched it.

He needed to keep it safe.

I watched a long time.

CHAPTER 51.1

He woke up.

He was on the ground.

It was dark.

Where was he?

Who was he?

He sighed.

He would die soon.

He felt the cold, clammy, claustrophobia of death entering his body.

He would never see it.

The letter was killing him.

He could not endure such happiness.

Kotan lie there — unable to move — and cursed the day he was born.

What kind of world was he born to?

Why was he born at all?

His Fate was Suffering.

CHAPTER 51.2

The dogs take turns sniffing butts.

"What the hell have you been eating, Barry?"

"Oh, it's a new healthy mix." Barry spoke casually.

Marvin suddenly barked. "You're eating that veggie crap!"

Barry protested. "No! No! It's an organic mix..."

But Marvin insisted. "You're a freaking vegetarian! You're no dog!"

Barry's ears drooped, and he muddled away like poor Eeyore.

Dogs were the worst bullies.

CHAPTER 51.75

Joe was too brash, too cocky. In the West, those kind of men died or quickly moved on. With Joe it was the former.

Dad was a preacher man in Missouri. Mum tried to keep track of her 14 children, but Joe needed more excitement, and at 15 he caught up with a wild group headed West. They found themselves at odds with the law, and steadily built a sour reputation.

In Kansas Joe killed his first man. Egged on by his companions, he picked a fight at a bar with a local farmer. The man had a wife and seven children. He had stopped in for a drink before heading home for the day.

It was the last thing he ever did.

He had a steady hand, but he was slow, and they buried him under a cottonwood just north of town. His wife was making bear sign for their anniversary, and he had been anticipating it for a month.

She waited up all night, pacing, feeling the terror of the unknown.

They drew straws in the morning; Billy Tinfeld and Sal Picker lost. Tinfeld was the hostelry man and blacksmith on the East side of town, a solid man who stood by his work. Picker owned the general store. They rode out to the farm, dismounted, removed their hats, and relayed the farmer's Fate in a few words to the farmer's widow. A couple of the children stood by, wide-eyed. Picker went to his saddle, and returned with a small sack of silver coins, and the farmer's boots, hat, and gun.

"Figured you should at least have these."

She listened, asking few questions. Her face was haggard and puffy from a sleepless, tearful night. Many more would follow. Tinfeld never forgot what she looked like, nor how he felt that day. Picker looked glum.

They rode back in silence.

In Colorado Joe killed his second. That one, many argued, deserved it. He was a ne'er-do-well, a tinhorn, a gambler. Joe thought he cheated. Nobody knew whether he did or not, but they knew well enough he had before. The price for his sins came due, and they buried him on Boot Hill.

By this time Joe was known as a gunfighter and started strutting around with his gun tied down. He heard there was a feud up in Montana and decided to hire his gun. It beat dusty cattle work. In Bozeman he received a letter from home. He was slow with letters, but after a few days he worked it out. His older brother was mayor in the town he was born. Another brother went east and became a lawyer. His sister married another preacher in town. The family was thrilled. They loved him and prayed for him every day.

The letter hit like a bolt of lightning, and suddenly he decided to quit.

It was time to grow up.

The next day he was packing his horse, and Frank Tally accosted him. Frank was a tough man, and he never liked

Joe. Joe for his part realized what a fool he had been. He had made enemies, but it was too late.

"What's the matta, Joe? Leavin so soon?"

He smirked.

"You yella?"

Joe put a bullet in Frank's leg, but took one in the heart.

His family never heard the story.

His bones are still there, somewhere, part of the rugged Montana soil. The wood marker above him soon disappeared. Somebody dug him up for his boots; his guns and horse were auctioned off. His belt buckle remains somewhere in the dirt, where it will remain for a long time.

In the West the price for sin was death.

But the truth was even more simple.

Live by the gun. Die by the gun.

CHAPTER 52.1

He emerged from the gloom. His face was dark and strangely intense.

She felt suddenly frightened. In his presence she felt a familiar alarm, and her soul shivered.

"The baby has to go."

He quietly choked. His voice strained at every word.

She silently hyperventilated.

He approached.

Terrified, she turned and fled his gaze.

She would never stop running. She never could. She dared not.

She would have the baby.

If it were the last thing she did.

CHAPTER 52.2

Finally in another world, she briefly paused.

She now knew what it was she felt.

She had tried to convince herself it was guilt.

But it was fear.

She rubbed her belly, reassuring her baby — in reality, reassuring herself.

"It's alright, Kotan. It's alright."

CHAPTER 52.3

Inyoku loved her husband.

She knew he would never understand her guilt, how terribly she felt for her malfeasance.

How could he?

But she never meant to hurt anybody.

Only one thing could resolve her stress. Only one thing made her forget. Only one thing could blunt the horrors of this life, only one thing could give her a glimpse of a better future, the slightest hint of pleasure in a barren and fruitless life.

It was a Curse.

She did not mean to hurt him, but that only made it worse. In fact she was eternally grateful for his compassion and generosity. He had saved her.

She had to do it.

As long as she had life, she had to. It was life itself. Was there a choice or was there not? Did it matter?

Her Fate was Suffering.

CHAPTER 52.4

He wanted to die. He felt like there should be something warm from the past, something that stopped him from dying, but... the past was cold.... The pleasant memories from his life had turned into a gnawing cancer.

He felt desperate for some sort of love, but there was nothing. From anybody. He was despised, rejected, and betrayed, and there was no sense chasing it now. It was over. Not even his friend truly loved him, because she was incapable of love.

He only loved people who did not know how to love in return.

What was wrong with him?

Or rather, what was not wrong with him?

CHAPTER 53

Jeff, my favorite neighbor, walked up to my front door one day and pulled a gun on me.

"I'm gonna kill you, Sanchez!" He shouted wildly.

"My name's not Sanchez." I calmly replied.

"F*** you, Sanchez!"

Ignoring this outburst, I shushed him.

Frantically.

"You are making a scene!"

Suddenly Jeff crumpled over.

I heard the shot.

Cherubini, the neighbor I hated, had gunned him down.

I looked down at Jeff.

Poor Jeff.

The neighbor I (no longer) hated winked and gave me the thumbs up.

I reciprocated.

He doffed his cap and mopped his brow.

"Hot'n today, ain't it?"

"Sure is!" I replied cheerfully.

He had earned a week of unconditional validation.

I was slightly annoyed the man I hated was a hero.

I had liked Jeff.

Why did nice guys always turn out to be deranged killers?

CHAPTER 53.9

Kotan thought they had a special connection.

Until he saw her around others.

Turns out everybody had a special connection with her.

He was a fool.

But it was too late.

One could never really reverse a marriage. A divorce could never undo the past. And a divorce... was there really such a thing? They were connected forever, whether or not any love remained.

CHAPTER 54.1

Kotan took a deep puff on one of his Cubans. He had picked the box himself on a trip to Cuba, and the rum beside him on the table.

"There is no good rum outside of Cuba." He informed his friend.

They talked about nothing and enjoyed the sunshine.

His friend was one he had always loved, somebody he wished he could know better, but somebody he knew he could never be with forever. Like every woman he ever loved. Including his wife.

He had never loved somebody that could work, somebody that would be a good match — only those that would destroy him in the end. She was his best friend, and everyday he lived in fear and dread of that moment she found somebody, and their relationship would change forever. Somehow the idea that they were both single made everything work. It was not sexual tension, but a truer form of intimacy... that could never be... Somehow you were never free enough when one party was spoken for.

Was he spoken for?

Was she?

How he longed to be closer! How he longed to be with her more! To see her again and again. How he wished he could keep chasing her around the world forever. That brief moment when they sat down together... that was the only thing mattered... he could find no way to express the value, other than that he would stop at nothing...

He watched her closely. What a satisfaction to see the way her face looked, the way her lips looked, her chin.... He studied the blemishes on her skin.... not with judgement, but with a deep desire to know.... He needed to know each and every one. He had to know everything. Everything he possibly could.

He basked in her presence.

And he listened to her talk, to the pacing and inflection of her words. He noticed all of her clothings and accessories. The way she waved her hands when she talked. The curves of her neck. And, yes, all the other curves....

Kotan chuckled as he realized that love made the most self-absorbed person — like himself — into the most observant. Normally he noticed nothing. The bomb that exploded and destroyed the building he was in? It meant nothing. The sirens behind him? What were they in this world? The gunfire to his left? Why bother looking? Who cared?

To love a friend was the most painful experience in life. And sadly he only loved his friends, never his enemies. He was too smart to follow Romeo, and yet the impossible love of a friend was worse than the impossible love of an enemy. Far worse.

There was nobody else to blame. No war. No circumstance. No parents. No religion.

Only he himself.

He flagellated himself, without mercy, and suffered gravely every moment of every day. He cried and he screamed, but he could never take the step toward what was called a relationship. He could never do it.

Was it because Fate did not allow it?

Did it matter?

It would never happen, and he would die alone and miserable. The people that waited on him in the hospital or nursing home would hope and pray that he would hurry up and die. He would do his best. With respect.

Love to him was warmth. Respect was affirmation, and the moment she told him she appreciated him, he almost died with ecstasy. He went black: he saw nothing; he felt nothing... it was something like panic.... A moment of intense discomfort followed, but she quickly noticed that he could not process it or handle it, and adeptly steered the conversation elsewhere. He loved her for noticing, for bailing him out, for helping him. It was a sign of more respect.

He married the wrong woman.

How did it happen? She did it all, and he merely went along — it was the modern story of Eden. Nothing had changed since the beginning: the stories were the same, generation after generation — he was following a pattern deeply ingrained in his flesh for thousands of years. Memories he knew before he was born.

"I traveled the world for many years." He paused. "One thing I learned. The world is a very dark place. Every money changer, every taxi driver, every airline, every store, every vendor, every government, every hotel, every public transportation system..... all of them, all of them are looking for ways to take advantage of you, to get the better of you, to extract what they can. Nobody is looking out for you.

Nobody. The only disappointment anyone has if you die is that they cannot coax more from you... but in the end, they do not even care about that, because they have already moved on to others..."

She nodded.

He felt even more in love with her. He liked how she often seemed to agree with him. He liked that she seemed to listen. All he ever wanted in life was somebody to listen to him. Especially somebody young and beautiful.

"They enact their revenge on other people: sometimes the land, sometimes animals... They harm life.... They are poison, and the poison affects us all, coming from a deep bitterness from within their souls that springs into the opposition of all that is good, because that sort of darkness can never coexist with light."

She listened.

"Cheers." she said. "To the end of such creeps."

"To the end of such creeps."

Their eyes met, and it felt like love.

The ancient kind, the kind that had died out long before they realized who they were, where they came from, or where they were headed.... maybe, just maybe... was there... could it be??? Their hearts beat, and leapt into their lungs, as they stole shallow breaths; their words froze before they could be uttered... and they stared in amazement, unable to blink, in perfect understanding of the other, trying to make the moment last, fearing when this would end... it would end... they knew it had to end.... but they stayed together... they held each other.

Maybe they could stay there forever.

Life was Suffering.

CHAPTER 55.4

He remembered the handwriting on the wall, and it still resonated. But he was slowly reconsidered his life motto. In the end did it matter what he believed? Or did it matter what he did?

CHAPTER 55.5

He finally understood.

Because it is difficult to have both, it is better to have time than money.

It was the sort of thing one learned right before dying.

CHAPTER 55.6

Whenever Kotan saw a falling star, it was always the same.

Most people wished, but he begged; he pleaded; he cried out.

Just one second like it used to be.

Just one.

He longed for those moments they were in love.

CHAPTER 55.8

Two basset hounds slyly approached each other.

"Hey Richard, I've got 3 grams."

"Sorry Edgar, I'm laying off. You know I get too wild after a hit."

"That's because you're using the wrong stuff." He winked.

"Sorry. Edgar, I'm done."

He quickly turned ugly and growled.

"Don't mess with me, Richard! You know the dogs I run with."

CHAPTER 56

Kotan shrugged. "It was from somebody who claimed to be my cousin. Said he was passing through and wanted to see me."

"Sounds suspicious."

Kotan appeared thoughtful.

"A cousin from which side?"

"I never knew any from my dad's side. They hate each other."

"They are after money."

Kotan shrugged.

Who was not?

CHAPTER 57.9

"You would not remember me, but I remember when you were born like yesterday."

Kotan nodded.

"I have heard that before."

"Of course." He paused. "So what has your life been like?"

Kotan shrugged.

"Normal."

"You have money." He pointed out.

Shrug.

"I never knew it."

"And now?"

"I do not care for it."

"Why? What about travel?" He paused. "Women?"

Kotan waved a hand.

"Dead to me."

"What is not dead?"

"Nothing."

"Is it your mom?"

"What do you mean?"

"What you're hiding. You're hiding something."

Kotan wanted to leave, but he also wanted to explore his fear for the first time.

"You knew my mom?"

"Of course."

Kotan sat very still, afraid to move.

"Tell me everything."

"She was very fierce, very strict. We were terrified of her."

He half-laughed, and continued more soberly.

"Your father adored her. He never recovered."

"I know."

"When she died —

"How did she die????" Kotan blurted.

"What?????" His cousin recoiled in shock.

The barista snuck a quick glance while casually wiping the counter.

Silence.

"....You mean... You never knew?"

He spoke in measured tones.

Kotan squeezed and unsqueezed his fingers.

"She died giving birth to you."

"That's a lie."

Kotan suddenly crumpled over, slid off his chair and hit the ground with a thud.

His cousin rushed over.

It was messy.

Very messy.

CHAPTER 58

A successful funeral was one where everybody cried.

This one was too sad for tears.

Father's ashen face plummeted to the depths, and he finally understood the curse upon him.

He had nobody left in this world, because he had murdered his own family.

Life was Suffering.

CHAPTER 58.1

"One thing is for sure."

He informed her.

"Generous people never do well financially... They cannot! Wealth has to invest in itself... it has to build.... Impossible to have values and be wealthy..."

He grew passionate.

"Why should we ever assume otherwise about the rich?"

She smiled and kissed him playfully.

"You are rich, dear."

He deliberately ignored her.

"Your wealth is in relation to your empathy. The more empathy you have, the less money.... The more you care about people, the less money you will have....

"This is the way of the world..."

He declared solemnly, bowing his head from the weight of Truth.

She sighed, but played along. "True. True.... What you believe about money defines you..."

He jolted with surprise. He stood up quickly, and clutched his throat, and pawed his forehead, and scratched his ear frantically. His eyes became like those of an eagle's, and he saw her for the first time. For the first time, his eyes penetrated her.

Deeply troubled, he pondered where Wisdom came from. His brow furrowed. Maybe she knew something. Maybe she... He paused... it was almost as if... as if she... He dared not even think it... it was too...

He wished he had married her. Not the woman he was cursed with. But it was over.... There was only one life.... one life, and one wife.

CHAPTER 58.2

The little boy shook his head sadly. "I do not fit in this world." He uttered morosely. "I thought they were my friends, but they ignored me."

"All of my friends ignore me too. I have none."

"This world is not my home." He added.

The boy nodded. "Then where is your home?"

"The next life."

He did not bother telling him that home was complicated.

Home is childhood itself.

Or adulthood itself.

Life itself.

Home is where you live, or where you want to live. Home is with family, or with friends, or maybe with yourself, as you extend your hands over a crackling fire in late autumn, near the friend you love but could never know the way you wanted to.

Your parents, or not your parents. Your wife, or not your wife.

Your children.

What children?

Who had those anymore?

So he patted the boy on the head, and walked on, ceaselessly, tirelessly, still looking for something, still looking for someone, still fighting his Fate.

CHAPTER 58.3

"A table in the sun please."

"The sun? It is much too hot, Signor!" The waiter was amazed.

"The Sun and I are best friends — I can handle her for at least an hour. My other friends... never!"

The waiter stared.

The only thing he ever wanted in life was to sunbathe for two to three hours a day in the tropics. It was the only thing that made him happy. It was the only thing he count on. Nothing else mattered.

Kotan wagged his head.

The waiter understood very little about life.

CHAPTER 58.33333333

Inyoku laughed. The sound of her laugh was like Beethoven's Ode to Joy. It never ceased to draw his affection.

"Everybody has a love-hate relationship with sex, right? We love orgasm and hate everything else."

Why did he not see it?

Infatuation was the most dangerous thing in the world.

Nothing else was close.

CHAPTER 58.4

The young man slowly walked through the beautiful square. Saturday night. Summer. Packed with all sorts of people and excitement. He passed by group after group, full of jollity. The more groups he saw, the more he realized he had nobody to belong to, no groups, no people.

Nowhere to go.

He stumbled around like the Wandering Samurai. Was he only lost now? Or lost forever? In eternal darkness?

He walked around the square again.

What was the point?

He returned home and stared at his phone all night.

He felt miserable. Yet he could see no way out. There was no hope in this life. Nowhere to turn. He was born to suffer, born to die. That was the way of it, and that trajectory overrode every thought, every purpose — there was only the Sword of Damocles, hanging o'er his head. Soon it would fall. Very soon.

He grew suddenly impatient, almost angry.

Let it. Let it right now.

His life was an epic disaster, an epic failure. Only Virgil

or Cecil could understand, the great poets of old. Nobody now knew the romance of suffering, or the merits of virtue. Nobody was left that knew of that great civilization.

Soon he would die.

It would be over.

Kotan was too wise. He understood that the key to living was to be preoccupied with death. One had to know where he was headed.

He had to plan.

But he never planned.

He was never fit for this life. The experts looked at him, and gave him a list of his options. None of them paid anything; none of them offered a way out. There was no hope. None. Nobody could offer a path.

CHAPTER 58.5

Kotan never slept well when his alarm was set.

Restless, anxious all night.

"When I get rid of this..."

He gestured to his phone.

"I will finally have rest."

"You will never have rest."

She was too truthful. He loved her for telling the truth, but despised her for not being sensitive to what he was saying.

He sighed.

An earnest prophesy among friends is always right.

"You sound like you have been there."

"In my dreams... I have..." She looked starry and angelic.

"Oh! How do you know about Timbuktu?"

"It is a long story."

"Okay."

".... About love, betrayal, death, and hope.... about a different world than the one we inhabit..... about the past and the future."

"Everything about the past is about the future... the

future is about the past... The only way to make sense of it is to lose your senses, and the only way to love it is to hate it...."

"..... and the only way to see is to be blind."

"The only way to walk is by crawling...."

They locked eyes.

CHAPTER 58.6

A few names came flooding back.

Most of his life was forgotten, most of it fuzzy, and he was certain of nothing anymore.

But he never forgot any of his crushes.

He knew every name from every stage of his life. He went through each one, and thought about them, what he knew, what he thought he knew.... and above all wondered what might have been....

With her.

Or her, even her.

Every one that made him feel Something. Every girl that excited his Imagination.

They all held a place Forever.

He knew them All.

Did they ever consider him? Did they ever dream about him?

Maybe there was the slightest thought, the slightest trigger, from some deep, forgotten past, and for a moment they had a spark of curiosity....

No.

None of them ever did.

None of them cared.

Deep down he knew the truth.

Other people moved on, and very quickly, but he never did. He never figured out how to move forward. He only felt the past, replaying and reliving memories never quite real, ghosts haunting an otherwise tepid life, obsessing over what might have been. Always afraid of losing something precious. Always fighting nature, a nature that obscured that which was, blurring the past into murky oblivion... bit by bit... darkness overwhelming the scene, until lost forever in the blackness....

Why remember?

Why the torture?

The one night he should have made a move. He had thousands of options now, what he ought to have done, what he wish he could try now, but it was too late.

It was all over.

He suddenly remembered his classmate that died.

What would her life have been like?

He felt somehow he should be more thankful for the time he had, but somehow he felt too restless, like nothing ever worked, like nothing had ever lined up for him, like he had not improved anybody else's life.

The oldest memories were harder to understand. He could no longer see his childhood. His childhood teachers.... their faces were disappearing... he had no idea what his voice sounded like or those of his friends... he had spent years at that school, but no memories... all gone... and the past became more and more mysterious... he became more and more a stranger to himself.

Who was he?

How could he know?

He had forgotten.

His past self could never have foreseen him.

And he could never again recognize who he was.

If he had no understanding of himself, who he was, who he is, or who he would be, how could he expect to understand anybody? How could he expect to know anybody beyond the briefest glint, beyond the most temporary moment?

He heard the story of her life. He listened. He tried to remember the details, but none of them seemed to matter. They were part of her — but what part of her?

He knew life was almost over.

He knew his time was almost up.

How did he feel?

He hoped he had made a difference in somebody's life.

Maybe one person?

But as Death came for him, he had doubts.

In the end it all came down to Faith.

CHAPTER 58.7

The biggest sin is forgetting.

As he aged he became more sinner, less saint. He lost more and more of the past. He could no longer remember everybody; he had less love to give; less attention to give; the two were the same...

It meant more now, if he received a message or a card — every year that went by, the more he should have been forgotten... if somebody remembered, it was more of a treasure, more precious, and far more surprising....

How about her? How did she think of him? Now, after all these years? The cares of life multiply over the years.... the demands on our attention... the captivity of life...

A single unsolicited note was better than all the riches of the world.

He saved every handwritten note he ever received. He considered they were the summary of his life: notes from family, friends, lovers... graduation cards, birthday cards, just-because cards — everything.

Somehow he never wanted anybody to see them. He wanted them all destroyed. He wanted to keep them as long as he had life and breath, but he needed them to die with him.

At the same time, he wished somebody would care about him enough to find them and save them. But that was foolish. He had to destroy his pride. He had to destroy that selfishness before he died. He had to get rid of that notion that he needed to be remembered. It was wrong.

If he lost touch with his past, the past was worthless. Why did he live it? Why did he live it with such nihilistic passion?

There was nothing if it were forgotten.

The biggest sin is forgetting.

CHAPTER 58.9

He opened the letter, and he read it.

As the words made contact with his soul, he became increasingly agitated. The card shook; the sound of it wobbling reverberated through the air. A large tear hit the card and blurred some of the ink. He quickly held the card out further, as more tears plummeted toward the earth. Everything was blurry. When he reached the end, he realized the climax of his life had arrived, the decision point — nothing before nor after mattered. His Fate boiled down to this one thing, down to one request from an old friend, who also happened to be the one he truly loved, the one whom he adored, the only one that could touch him with a single look, with a single word. Rick had all night to think about Ilsa, but time meant nothing now. Nothing. He had always known his Fate, and so had Ilsa. What was an hour, a year? His whole life everybody else had made his decisions. For the first time he would make his own.

CHAPTER 59.1

"The baby has to go."

He spoke very calmly.

She shook her head sadly, feeling genuine guilt at what she was doing, and realizing her Fate was sealed from this moment forever.

"No."

He turned and left.

CHAPTER 59.2

As he walked through the house for the last time, he passed through his son's room and noticed his wife's handwriting. He had forgotten that it was there. Maybe he never knew.

He sagged to the floor and wept.

She was wrong.

It had nothing to do with money.

THE END

Kotan walks in.

He pulls out a knife and throws it across the room. Strike. The man paws at it, gurgles, and dies.

His wife rushes him, screaming. They struggle violently, before he conclusively pins her down. Their faces are close and sweaty. She pleads and whimpers, whispering his first name. He sees the past in her eyes, but it is too late. He impales her with a knife, and patiently watches her die, convulsing and sputtering, blood on her lips.

He says nothing. His face reveals nothing.

He walks into the other room and moves a few things around to tidy up. He sees a couple dishes on the counter, washes them, dries them carefully, and puts them away. He takes his wallet out and throws it in the trash.

Checks his phone messages.

Responds to one.

"LOL."

Another one.

"I'm pretty slammed today. How about next week?"

Deletes a few emails.

Powers it off. Throws it away. Removes his wallet from the trash and pulls out the cash. He finds an envelope and places the cash inside. On the outside of the envelope, he writes, "To Sydney, With Love", and signs it.

He pulls out his phone again, and violently crushes it to pieces with a hammer. Then scoops what is left of it back into the trash can. He appears thoughtful. He sighs and feels relief like he has never felt.

One more thing.

He disappears in the bedroom and returns with a picture of the two of them in Zanzibar. They are flushed with happiness and joy, their cheeks touching, full of zest for life and the incomparable exhilaration of young love.

He takes the photo from the frame, blankly stares at it, and slowly tears it in half.

Disposes it.

Time passes.

He sits cross-legged in the middle of the room. He understands his Fate, and waits. His legs and back ache. At last he slowly pulls himself up and walks over to Inyoku. He watches her for an eternity.

He always thought he would go first.

But she mastered the art of being difficult.

For the last time in his life, he feels the throbbing presence of tears behind his eyes.

For the last time in his life, they were wrong.

They were wrong about everything.

His meditation over, he sits in the appointed place, and ceremoniously draws a beautiful samurai blade.

He has a silly thought.

Somewhere, somehow, Tarantino is beaming...

And Kobayashi...

And Shakespeare...

EPILOGUE

The man slowly lifted his glass. His hand trembled. He did not know whether to believe in Karma. He took a sip. Yet he knew, he always knew he had despised his son.

His wife.

Now his son.

He bowed his head.

Why not him? Why did he tarry?

He would tip millions.

Why not? Who else would get his money now?

The emperor?

The waitress appeared.

"Everything alright, sir?"

He stared at nothing.

"No. And it never will be."

She waited silently.

There was nothing to say.

ABOUT THE AUTHOR

I write satire and social commentary, building out stories from personal observations and insights, not from story boards. My controversial style of storytelling demands a lot of readers, but at the same time, I take care that each bite is digestible, if the whole is often shrouded in mystery. It is the same in life: why not in art? Everybody can take something away, and in life, and in art, we have to learn to appreciate what we do not understand.

W.C.